A Safe Place
Half Dead Novella
E.M. Lacey

Seeds of Fiction LLC

A Safe Place

A Half-Dead Novella

E.M. Lacey

* * *

* * *

Author's Note: This is a work of fiction. Names, characters, places, and incidents are a product of the author's imagination. Locales and public names are for atmospheric purposes. Any resemblance to actual people, living or dead, or to businesses, companies, events, institutions, or locales are completely coincidental.

Edited by *There For You Editing* and *Edit for Indies*

Cover Design by Book Cover by Design

ISBN: 978-1-963496-06-2

contents

ACKNOWLEDGMENTS

THIS IS THE SECOND edition, which includes adjustments to the prose. Thanks for the feedback on the initial release of "A Safe Place."

As always, it takes more than an idea to produce a book. You need friends, editors, cheerleaders, artists to get a book done. It doesn't hurt to sit at the feet of seasoned writers. I'd like to thank Melissa Ringsted of "*There for You Editing*" and Gabriella West of "*Edits for Indies*" for making my story shine. Thank you, Kellie Dennis of Book Cover by Design, for the amazing cover. Thank you to Ashley Cestra and Theresa Raimonde for your feedback. Finally thank you readers for picking up this book.

As always if there are any errors in this piece, they're mine.

Enjoy

Chapter 1

WELCOME TO THE NEW WORLD

0845 HOURS — DOWNTOWN Chicago, Illinois

They'd slept in an old office building, deciding to follow the Pink Line "L" tracks all the way to downtown Chicago at sunrise. Rather than walk the streets, which were too wild, the woman, two children, and their dog took the elevated tracks of the L. There was no electricity, so the tracks were safe. It had taken them a few hours to walk from the west side to the State and Lake Street stop, which overlooked the now-decrepit Chicago Theatre. Mrs. Morrison stood under the L-stop enclosure, hands cupped over her brow, blocking the sun, which shouldn't have been that bright so early in the morning, but so much had changed since the Morpheus Strain took root.

Nature thrived in the absence of men, transforming downtown into a literal urban jungle. Wildlife had moved into the city. Rabbits, deer, coyotes, and even horses roamed the streets. Mrs. Morrison, her children, and other travelers profited from the abandoned urban gardens, which were now as wild as the creatures moving about on four legs. Mrs. Morrison had come across a few wild apple trees and cornfields, and had managed to catch, and discreetly kill, a few chickens. The middle of State Street was a strip of crisp green grass, all of it tall. A gust of wind whipped through, causing a burst of flower petals to take to the air. Mrs. Morrison's gaze fell to the cinnamon-brown pit bull at her side, Sugar.

Sugar liked to chase the swirling flower petals. Mrs. Morrison wanted to grin at the intensity on Sugar's face as her eyes followed the rainbow-colored petals' dancing above the grass. A few twirled just beyond the tracks where they stood, but Sugar was a good girl and stayed put. They couldn't afford to get separated, not when they were so close to the rendezvous point.

Mrs. Morrison sniffed the air just as the wind passed, searching for alien smells, and even the familiar ones. The wind was stale, which was a good sign. Maybe they would make it to their destination without incident, so she signaled for the kids to come out of hiding.

A little brown boy, no older than six years old, crept out of the old information booth of the station. He tugged on the straps of his Kung Fu Panda backpack, tightening them before joining Mrs. Morrison and Sugar. A second child emerged. The buzz cut, and black-on-black clothing complete with matching elbow- and knee pads, made gender a tricky thing to figure out, but the pink Hello Kitty vest screamed girl. Hope was that: a girl.

Mrs. Morrison wasn't sure about Hope's age. During the Morrison family's travels through the decaying world, she and her husband Grant had discovered Hope in a house they were squatting in for the night. Hope hadn't spoken a word to anyone since they found her, but she trusted the Morrison family enough travel with them. The only reason Mrs. Morrison knew Hope's name was because of the name plates on the bedroom doors of the house. It turned out that she was not only the sole survivor, but also the only girl child in the family. Mrs. Morrison glanced down at Hope, her mouth tilted in a smile, she'd always wanted a daughter.

"We don't have much time, so we move quick and quiet." Mrs. Morrison spoke while scanning the street below for a route. "We'll hit State Street." Mrs. Morrison moved toward the turnstiles, of which there were three, testing each for functionality. Two were rusted in place. Lucky for them, at least one still worked.

Beep. Beep.

Mrs. Morrison's watch, a *Rangeman GW9400-3*, chirped, prompting her to check the time. It was almost 0900 hours. It left them with less than thirty minutes to get to the location Sergeant Carter had given her. She checked the compass. It was safer for them to use State Street. It was pretty straightforward. Wabash, which was always undergoing construction, was a maze that had way too many hiding places for her comfort.

Mrs. Morrison looked at her son, Joshua; the little guy had bags under his eyes. She'd heard his stomach growl a few times just before they crossed the lake. They'd run out of fresh food a day ago and were low on canned goods. Mrs. Morrison knew the journey had been hard on Joshua and Hope, but they managed to keep up. She offered the kids a smile. Joshua smiled weakly while Hope just nodded her head.

"Okay. We move like the ghosts of the Flash."

The Flash reference got a genuine smile out of Joshua. His backpack had a few Flash comic books inside. Mrs. Morrison pushed through the turnstile, followed by her children. Sugar slunk under it as they descended to State Street.

0910 Hours — Michigan Avenue and Erie

Mrs. Morrison crouched low, pressing her body close to the dusty wall of an old Apple store. She scanned the area, taking in the wilted lilies, dust-coated statues, bus stops, and benches. The streets of downtown Chicago were still crowded with a range of cars from rolling scrap heaps to high-end luxury vehicles; only they were all empty. Doors hung open. There were keys still in the ignition of most. The eeriest thing about the scene around her was that there was not a corpse to be found; no skeletons draped over steering wheels, lying in the middle of the streets, or sidewalks. People didn't die anymore. They went to sleep and when they woke, they were something else.

Reborn was what the media called those afflicted with the Morpheus Strain, which had surfaced back in 2018 when civilization circled the toilet. In the beginning, doctors thought it was a reaction to a new batch of immunizations against the ever-mutating flu. The infected complained of headaches, fevers, and aches in muscle joints, which progressed to seizures, problems with speech, and facial paralysis.

The symptoms led doctors to believe that a mutated form of encephalitis had surfaced, but they were way off base with their diagnosis.

Overnight, Johnsonville, a small town in Central Florida, showed signs of infection. Victims exhibited all the symptoms of encephalitis, only a bit more extreme. People wandered around, eyes glazed, movements lethargic, and no signs of coherent thought. A ten-car pile up on I-95 sounded the alarm. It was when the first responders and the media arrived that all hell broke loose. The wounded started biting their rescuers. In the next 72 hours, the medical teams, members of the media, along with the citizens of Johnsonville showed signs of infection. On the fourth day, the government stepped in and quarantined the whole town, but it was already too late.

The Morpheus Strain was a mutation. All attempts to counter it failed. It changed too quickly for doctors to cure. It was undetectable through medical testing. The virus had been engineered to imitate the chemical qualities of whatever vaccine it occupied. No one knew who was infected until much later. For some, change was immediate. For others, it took a few days, months, or years, but one thing was certain, the virus took over eventually. All a carrier had to do was hit REM sleep. Soon it was discovered that a single bite could accelerate and warp the mutation. It wasn't long before people began to fear sleep and each other. Four years later, the new American Dream had become one of survival, and even that was hard.

A squall tore through the empty streets, taking on a ghostly howl. Several cars shook violently, creating dust clouds. Mrs. Morrison froze, cocking her head toward the mouth of the alley that hid them. She pressed the crown of her head to the garbage dumpster she and the kids huddled behind and listened. She thought she heard something other than the wailing wind.

Someone was talking. It was hard to hear, since the mutterer was barely speaking above a whisper. The slow slide of feet along the pavement paused. Its breathing was ragged. It said something...no...*she* said something. It was a woman and she sounded drunk. Her words slurred.

"Puuummshhinn. Puuummshhinn, coommmee baaack." The muttering was faint but edging closer.

Was she a survivor?

Mrs. Morrison spared a glance at the frightened children beside her. She offered them a quick smile before her eyes slid back to the ground beneath the dumpster. She would at least be able to see the shadow of the person or thing approaching them. Sugar growled low. Mrs. Morrison put her finger up to her mouth and the dog quieted.

The shuffling feet stopped.

"Puuummshhinn," the woman whispered louder then the shuffling feet headed into their alley.

Mrs. Morrison tapped her head. The children pulled down the visors of their motorcycle helmets. The first thing on Mrs. Morrison's end of the world agenda was getting her family outfitted for survival. Mrs. Morrison and Grant didn't wait for things to get bad before they started making preparations. Grant hit up the local sporting goods stores while Mrs. Morrison went to a Harley-Davidson store for their basics: biker jackets, boots, helmets, and riding gloves. The visors offered their faces protection. She made sure they were tinted for their days in the sun. Seven months into the apocalypse, Wal-Mart was still standing. It was there that Mrs. Morrison stocked up on construction boots, sneakers, socks, jeans, and pullover shirts. The apocalypse was no friend to button-down shirts. Clothes needed to be a single-motion deal.

Mrs. Morrison pulled her expandable baton from its scabbard. She couldn't afford to spill blood, so she left her machete, Maxine, in its sheath, which was strapped to her back.

Joshua whimpered. Mrs. Morrison placed a fist over her heart and beat it lightly, three times against her chest. It was their sign to one another to take courage. Joshua nodded, closed his eyes, and began rocking a little.

Sugar bared her teeth but remained quiet.

The shuffling entered the alley. Sugar crouched lower, muscles bunched up, ready to spring. Mrs. Morrison held out her arm, palm open. Sugar sat upright, moving in front of the children, teeth still bared.

The shuffling was now very close to the dumpster. Mrs. Morrison pulled her arm up into the ready position, as the woman's dragging steps got closer.

The shuffling stopped.

"Pummmshhinn," the whispering woman said again. Mrs. Morrison saw the tip of a lavender leash swing in and out of view along the edge of the dumpster. It looked more like a noose than a leash, being that there was no dog attached to it. The shuffling started again. Mrs. Morrison snapped her baton to its full length and kneecapped the whispering woman. She hoped this one had brittle bones, you never knew with Reborns. The snap that resounded after the first hit put a smile on her face.

The undead were nothing like the movies, or television for that matter, Mrs. Morrison thought as she watched the woman fall. First, it was hard to label all of them as undead. There was still something very human about them. Reborns spoke very little, if at all. Some lumbered about like the woman on the ground, but there were others who had a spark of intelligence.

Mrs. Morrison used to think it was the uninfected playing dumb for the sake of survival, but that was not the case. They were *aware*. Maybe it was some trace of humanity—the soul—still trapped inside a diseased body. Mrs. Morrison had heard stories of comatose patients being aware of everything around them only they lacked the ability to respond; maybe that's what it was like to be Reborn.

Once, Joshua took a toy from a house they were in. The Reborn, a child, followed them. It got aggressive with Joshua a few times until Grant figured out what it was after. When Grant found out Joshua had taken a toy from the house, an action figure, he retrieved it, then placed it on the ground and stepped away. The Reborn approached, cautiously, eyes never leaving Grant. The moment it was close enough, it snatched the toy and went away. They never saw it again.

Mrs. Morrison studied the Reborn writhing on the ground. Its eyes were white—maybe it was blind—and its skin was a deep gray. It wore a pink shower cap, matching silk pajamas, and house slippers. Mrs. Morrison figured it was a resident of Mag Mile who probably lived in one of the luxury condominiums. Mrs. Morrison motioned for the kids to get up and prepare to run as she checked the alley for any more visitors.

Mrs. Morrison signaled Sugar to cover their rear as she moved to the front. They crept through the alley. Mrs. Morrison had her baton at the ready. All they had to do was make it past the Starbucks.

God, if you're still out there somewhere, please help me get my kids to safety, Mrs. Morrison prayed silently then looked up at the clear sky, resisting the urge to make the sign of the cross over her chest. Instead, she clutched the locket she wore, which held a picture of her family before the world ended.

Please, God, don't let him have followed us.

"Please," Mrs. Morrison whispered as she released her locket, gathered her courage, and then raised her right hand, fist clenched. The children stopped.

Mrs. Morrison padded forward, keeping close to the ground in case there were any Reborn around. Reborn were bad, but the quality of human beings that remained were worse. Most adults still living in the city, roaming the streets, were bad news. Those survivors who were trying to hang on to their humanity had learned to let go of possessions and stay on the move. This world required that everyone in a caravan be armed and combat-ready...even the children.

Mrs. Morrison sniffed the air, scenting neither the odor of spoiled milk nor the tangy scent of well-seasoned meat. Reborn reeked of spoiled milk, while the uninfected smelled like marinated meat just before it hit the grill.

Mrs. Morrison took a few bold steps forward, hanging near the rear of a Mercedes sedan. Poking her head out, she glanced in both directions. It was clear. She tapped the bumper three times. The kids and Sugar scurried to her side. Mrs. Morrison turned to them. Joshua looked like he was going to pop from being quiet for so long, but he was a trooper. Hope's eyes were focused on her, aware of every muscle tic, breath, and bead of sweat. Sugar sat beside Joshua, tongue lolling.

"Look, we've gotta get past that Starbucks," Mrs. Morrison explained, pointing at the empty building catty-corner from the Mercedes. "There are people waiting for us."

"Good people?" Joshua whispered.

"Good enough." She had decided that lying to kids was not an option when trust was what stood between life and death. "I don't know them, but there are doctors and soldiers."

Joshua didn't seem all that thrilled. Reaching out, Mrs. Morrison ran her finger along his cheek. "Listen, baby boy, I'm not gonna let anyone hurt you, and neither will Sugar, but we can't keep running on our own. We need a safe place, you know, where we can rest and not worry about looking over our shoulders."

Joshua wasn't convinced.

"You know, Josh, since the people in that building are doctors and scientists, they might find a way to make people better."

"Really?" Joshua's expression blossomed like a flower in the sun.

"I believe so." Mrs. Morrison looked away from Joshua and focused on their surroundings.

"That means they can fix—"

Holding up her hand, Mrs. Morrison cut him off. She knew where this conversation was going.

"Remember, I said they *might* be able to make people better."

Joshua's smile grew as he was amply satisfied with that answer.

"You ready?" she asked Joshua and Hope. Both of them nodded, then rolled into a runner's stance.

Mrs. Morrison used her hand as their stopwatch. She held up three fingers, ticked off one by one until there were none then they took off.

So far, they were in the clear as they turned the corner of the Starbucks on Erie and Fairbanks. Hope had just rounded the corner when Sugar slid to a stop. Sugar faced Fairbanks and started barking. *Not good.* The fur between Sugar's shoulder blades was standing on end and her muscles were tense; she was in full-on protective mode.

Joshua stopped, trembling, eyes wide, as he glanced back at Sugar. Mrs. Morrison had stopped as well. Men in military gear poured from the alley between Starbucks and the entrance to the hospital's loading area, automatic weapons at the ready.

Mrs. Morrison shushed Sugar. Her eyes were trained on the armed soldiers.

One soldier broke off from the mass, taking several steps forward then stopped. "Identify yourself." The soldier sounded young.

"Hope has arrived." Mrs. Morrison nodded toward Hope, who hid Joshua behind her.

The soldier lowered his weapon and relaxed his stance, though the soldiers behind him did not.

"I am Private Daniel Anderson, ma'am. Sergeant Carter informed us of your arrival."

The soldiers parted just as she heard a familiar growl.

"Go," she mouthed to Hope and Joshua. They ran toward the soldiers. Mrs. Morrison turned so she could see whatever was coming around the corner.

"Ma'am, we need to get you inside." Anderson held his hand out toward her.

Mrs. Morrison shook her head, heart sinking at the rapid tap of combat boots on asphalt.

"Ffaammiilleee!" Grant shouted, rounding the corner at full speed.

"Sugar, come!" Mrs. Morrison commanded, as she finally followed Anderson's advice and ran toward them.

"Please don't let Joshua hear or see him," she whispered to herself as she cleared the wall of soldiers. Sugar was right behind her.

"Daddy?" Joshua shouted as he twisted in the arms of the soldier who had grabbed him just as he began to run toward Grant.

"Damn it," Mrs. Morrison hissed under her breath. Joshua's voice would only set Grant off.

"Jooossshhheeee!" Grant snarled, slowing to a stalk. Grant was six-foot-four, all muscle, and none of it had deteriorated since he was bitten; if anything, it looked as if his skin was hardening. It had a gloss to it, very much like marble, but there were cracks in places. Grant was covered in police-grade body armor, which was all black. The only item of color on Grant was a strip of the baby blue T-shirt Joshua had gotten him for Father's Day. The word "Dad" waved like a banner on his left bicep.

Mrs. Morrison wondered if it was wrong to still consider him beautiful. Grant wore the body armor

well; it hid his tats, but accentuated his long, mus-
cled legs, broad shoulders, and well-defined arms.
It didn't help that the virus seemed to make those
damned baby blues glow. Mrs. Morrison had lost
her Grant nine months ago when he was bitten. She
was still having a hard time comprehending that the
man...no...the Reborn before her was not her husband. Her Grant had died to save them.

They had settled into an old daycare center,
much like the one Mrs. Morrison ran back in Tin-
ley Park. There was food, sleeping mats, and toys.
Joshua could never resist toys. What six-year-old
child could? They had settled in for the night when
Reborn surrounded the daycare. They must have
been older, because they were feral—bloodthirsty.
Grant cut himself to attract them. As soon as he bled
the Reborn were on him. Blood flowed in thin lines
across the floor, pooling between the bright colored
rubber floor mats shaped like puzzle pieces. Mrs.
Morrison watched her husband vanish under a pile of
Reborn. She couldn't remember how long she stood
there. It wasn't until the stream of blood touched her
boot that she took the kids and ran.

Mrs. Morrison thought the pack of Reborn had eat-
en him, but she was wrong. He walked away from it,
infected and obsessed. The one thing she learned
was that whatever had driven a Reborn in life, drove

them in death. Some people were greedy, territorial, cowardly, selfish, compassionate, and protective. In Grant's case, he was all about his family, which was Joshua, herself, and later Hope. Family was everything to Grant. So much so that he stalked them. He attacked anyone who got too close. Several times he approached them. He would stare at them. Nothing more.

The first thing everyone was taught at the beginning of the end was that carriers of the Morpheus Strain spread it through bites and scratches. Mrs. Morrison wondered if Grant would try to make them an eternal family by biting them. She didn't want to take that chance, so she ran with the kids. Joshua didn't understand why they ran away from Daddy. All she could tell him was that Daddy was sick and would get them sick.

"Ma'am!" Anderson called, snatching her from her thoughts. "We need you in here now!" He began to close the door.

Mrs. Morrison slipped past the soldiers lining the alley then entered the building.

"No!" Grant roared. "Faammmiillee!" Grant moved toward them and the soldiers opened fire. Grant's body shook from all the bullets, yet there was no real damage. The body armor he was wearing was doing its job. Mrs. Morrison watched Grant pull out the riot shield strapped to his back. Raising it, he charged the line of soldiers. The machetes he kept strapped to his back looked like a skewed crucifix. One machete was longer than the other. Grant also carried side arms. It seemed that even though the body went through death, the mind still kept its strongest skill, and for Grant that was killing. It was what he did as an Army Ranger.

"Let go of the door, ma'am," Anderson stated, jerking the door Mrs. Morrison was holding. She looked at her hand, which had a white-knuckled grip on the door's edge. Reluctantly, she released it. The door slid shut, but not she witnessed Grant grab one of the soldiers and snap his neck.

Mrs. Morrison turned to face the room of strangers. Two men in yellow Hazmat suits cautiously approached her. She backed toward the door. A tall, thin woman with wire-rimmed glasses watched her with big green eyes. She offered Mrs. Morrison a small smile.

"Please, miss," she said, her voice held a faint accent. "We do this to everyone, even our own when they return."

"I understand, you can't be too careful," Mrs. Morrison replied as she searched for her kids. Joshua sat in a corner clutching Sugar, who licked his face then turned a snarl toward the people in the small space they shared. Hope stood in front of Joshua and Sugar, her eyes, as always, laser focused on her new environment, searching for exits.

"Can you take four steps away from the door, ma'am?" One of the men in a Hazmat suit requested. Once Mrs. Morrison had taken the allotted number of steps, the second man moved behind her. She tensed, it was a reflex. She never liked anyone she didn't know moving outside of her range of sight.

"Please, ma'am, don't panic. We just need to check you for—*bite*!" The suited man shouted behind her.

The man behind Mrs. Morrison swept her feet out from under her. She let him. He pulled a black bag over her head as someone pinned her to the ground. She did not struggle. Someone zip-tied her wrists together and stripped her of her weapons. Joshua shrieked to her right. Sugar snarled. Shouts erupted. Mrs. Morrison felt a growl building before the world was silenced by noise-canceling headphones.

Chapter 2

UNDER THE MICROSCOPE

0928 Hours — Examination Room

Mrs. Morrison was not sure how long she'd been standing in the middle of the dark room. After the security team executed D.R.S. protocol—disable, restrain, and silence—the soldiers added shackles to her ankles during the elevator ride down, brought her to the room and then retreated to the recesses.

Mrs. Morrison tilted her head up, in the direction of the soft thrum of electricity. The vibration tickled her scalp. The hood dulled her sense of smell but didn't kill it. She could smell people. They weren't close, maybe several feet away from her on all sides. They reeked of chemicals and meat.

Mrs. Morrison wasn't sure what their game was, but she'd play along. She straightened her spine, lifted her chin, and did not move. They were afraid of her. She couldn't blame them. As far as they knew she was Reborn. Sure, she had been bitten, but Mrs. Morrison didn't feel like a Reborn. There were some changes since the bite. Her sense of smell was heightened, she no longer needed sleep, and she *knew* what was hers—her kids, her dog, and once upon a time, Grant. Even when she closed her eyes and pretended to sleep, Mrs. Morrison knew where Hope, Joshua, and Sugar were. She also knew that she didn't have much time to convince whoever she was going to meet that she was harmless, because in less than an hour she would go ballistic until her kids were returned. She wouldn't be able to help herself. It was an instinct thing.

Someone moved to her right. The fine hairs on her arms raised: not out of fear, it was a sensory thing. Tapping. It was to her left. Morse code? They were communicating with her.

May we approach?

Mrs. Morrison nodded.

Do not move. We will restore your hearing first, then sight.

Mrs. Morrison nodded her understanding.

You are surrounded.

Mrs. Morrison nodded a third time. She remained still as she felt the heat of an approaching body. The person stopped in front of her, looked away, most likely looking at the soldiers before turning back toward her. She felt the slight weight of hands settling on her earphones and then they were gone.

"I'm going to take your right arm now so I can guide you to the examination table." Mrs. Morrison recognized the voice. It was the woman from earlier, the one with the glasses and the accent.

The woman put her hand on Mrs. Morrison's bicep and pulled. Mrs. Morrison didn't budge.

"Please cooperate." The woman tugged Mrs. Morrison in the direction she wanted her to go.

"I'll move when you tell me what's going to happen to me on that table?"

Someone huffed from the shadows. "You're not in a position to ask questions or make demands."

Mrs. Morrison moved her head in the direction of the voice. It was haughty and well spoken, but there was a whine beneath it. The woman tapped Mrs. Morrison's arm gently.

"Please, we need to strap you down for the medical staff's safety."

"Is there another option?" Mrs. Morrison let the woman move her two steps before stopping again. "I don't want to... no...I can't handle being strapped down."

"Oh...but we have to..."

Mrs. Morrison sniffed the air. "You have men here with guns. All they have to do is put one in my brain and that should do it."

"Okay." The woman's hand fell from Mrs. Morrison's arm

"I will stand, with the mask off, and take whatever tests you want." The quicker she complied, the better it would be for her and the kids. She had to prove that she was no threat. Hopefully they, whoever *they* were, would believe her.

"That's a reasonable request," the woman replied.

Someone moved toward Mrs. Morrison from the right. She smelled gun oil and aftershave, then the bag was gone.

Mrs. Morrison blinked her eyes. The same tall, bespectacled woman she saw earlier was with her in the room with two of the original guards, Anderson and Kidd. The woman wore a simple gray dress, black flats and a lab coat.

"Where are my kids?" Mrs. Morrison asked as she scanned the room. It had a blue hue to it. Video screens lined the surrounding walls. She looked up. A thick black cable that she would not have been able to detect had she been uninfected was the source of the electric hum. This place, though electric power had gone out years ago, was running on more than a generator. Mrs. Morrison fixed her attention on the woman in front of her.

"The children are fine," the bespectacled woman with the dark hair paused, studying Mrs. Morrison before adding, "They are safe."

"How can I be sure of that?"

The woman pulled a remote from the pocket of her lab coat. She aimed it a screen then pressed a button. Hope, Joshua, and Sugar were all in what looked like a regular kids' bedroom. It had a Disney theme, Beauty and the Beast, on the walls, the lamps, and even the bedspread. Hope sat in the bed cradling Joshua in her arms. Sugar rested her head on Hope's thigh. Sugar lifted her head lethargically, which meant she had been sedated.

"Satisfied?"

Mrs. Morrison nodded then walked to the examination table, hopped on it, and lay back, folding her hands across her stomach.

"Tell us about Hope."

"Haven't you started testing her?" Mrs. Morrison arched her left brow, angling her head so they were eye to eye.

The woman chuckled. "Of course we've started testing. She has bite marks on her. They've healed, so how do we know that those are not from something else?"

"Those bite marks were on her when I found her."

"Those could have been from another uninfected person." The woman sniffed. She ran her fingers along her name badge, which read Mays, as if it were more interesting.

Mrs. Morrison laughed. The woman's hand froze over her badge then slowly descended to her side. "What's so funny?"

"You." Mrs. Morrison said, genuinely amused. She looked around the room, taking note of the seven people still concealed in the shadows. "You have been holed up in this place for a while. I know you haven't been twiddling your thumbs. Come on, you're scientists! I'm sure you've been researching, dissecting, and whatever you *people* do in the name of science."

Mrs. Morrison looked pointedly around the room again, pointedly pausing in the direction of each person still in the shadows. "Sergeant Carter told me you could help us. You knew we were coming and you want to play games," she snarled. "I told you I would submit to your tests. I'm obviously infected," Her voice hardened even more, becoming almost guttural. "Don't you want to know what makes me tick? Why am I aware?" Mrs. Morrison mocked.

Mays licked her lips.

"Was Sergeant Carter wrong and you can't help us?" Mrs. Morrison let disappointment seep into her voice.

"Of course we can," someone huffed to her right, but he didn't move from his hiding place.

Mrs. Morrison sucked her teeth and rolled her eyes. "Sure you can, that's why we're playing games rather than getting answers."

"Questions are how we find answers," Mays countered.

"Your questions are a smoke screen. All the tech in here." Mrs. Morrison jerked her chin in the direction of the monitors. "All the hardware." She motioned toward the visible armed guards. "We're playing twenty questions."

"We have nothing but time," the man in the shadows to her right countered.

Mrs. Morrison closed her eyes, feeling the chill of the virus swimming through her veins. She drew it forward, gnashing her teeth. Smells changed, people looked different now. They smelled like food mixed with gun metal, aftershave, and whatever floral splash Mays wore. There was a bit of pressure just above her eyes before she opened them.

"Christ!" the man shouted from the right as the clatter of raised guns bounced off the walls. "Look at her eyes. They're glowing like an infected."

Mays retreated a few steps. Anderson and Kidd moved in front of her, guns pointed in Mrs. Morrison's direction.

"I told you that already."

"You shouldn't be able to talk," the man to Mrs. Morrison's right stated.

"How would you know that?" Mrs. Morrison countered.

There was a low buzz of conversation coming from every direction.

"She's nothing like any of the others we've studied," someone whispered. Mrs. Morrison could feel their gazes on her as she shoved the virus down.

"What others?" Mrs. Morrison turned her head in the direction of the speaker.

"How can she hear us? The others showed no signs of consciousness, much less the enhanced hearing," someone hissed.

"I can hear you, smell you, and feel you," Mrs. Morrison stated.

The click of fingers on triggers resounded. Mays held up her hand. "No need for that." Mays looked at Mrs. Morrison, really looked at her as she took a few tentative steps closer. "Do you know your name?"

"My name is Esperanza Magdalena Morrison. I am thirty-seven years old. I owned a daycare. I lived near Governor's State University before the virus hit. My husband and I thought the suburbs would be a bet-ter place to raise our son, Joshua." Mrs. Morrison laughed at the irony of it all. "I guess nowhere is safe anymore."

"How are you still conscious?" Mays took a cau-tious step forward.

Mrs. Morrison shrugged.

"When were you bitten?"

"Six months ago."

There was a collective gasp in the room.

"That's unheard of," someone exclaimed.

"I thought once one is bitten that's it. The con-sciousness is lost. The body shuts down and does a sort of reboot and the resurrected result is a mind-less ischemic," the man in the shadows to her right said.

Mrs. Morrison pointed at the bite on her left be-tween her shoulder and neck. "Obviously, I was bit-ten." Then she pointed at her head. "The brains are still functional."

Mays's brow furrowed in confusion, "Why?"

Mrs. Morrison shrugged. "I can't afford to die. If I do, who's going to keep Joshua and Hope safe?"

The woman shared a look with the man in the shadows to her right.

"Amazing," someone whispered.

"We can keep them safe," Mays stated.

Mrs. Morrison shook her head. "No you can't. You're scientists."

"What's that got to do with anything?" the man in the shadows to her right said, sounding offended.

"You're clinical, not emotional. Besides you're too much of a coward to defend anyone," Mrs. Morrison sneered. "Children need your heart to be engaged."

"You're dead. You've got no heart," the man in the shadows to her right countered.

"Are you sure about that?" Mrs. Morrison asked, jerking her chin toward the stethoscope around Mays's neck.

Mrs. Morrison felt the man to the right of her move deeper into the shadows. Mays sucked her teeth and with a disgusted look, snatched up the stethoscope and moved forward.

"I'll do it, Baker, since you're too much of a coward."

Baker emerged from the shadows. He was a thin man, not too tall, with brown hair and bad skin. He wore a vest over a pressed white shirt under his lab coat. His black shoes were polished, and Mrs. Morrison was sure the rest of him was as well, at least on the outside.

"Look Mays, she's not exactly trustworthy. She's one of them," Baker thrust an accusatory finger at her.

Mays shook her head. "I don't think so." She approached Mrs. Morrison. "Do you mind?"

Mrs. Morrison shrugged. "Not at all."

After snapping on a pair of surgical gloves she pulled from her lab coat pocket, Mays moved the collar of Mrs. Morrison's shirt down enough so she could put the stethoscope over her heart. Mays's eyes stretched and her smile widened.

"Amazing," she whispered as she listened to the slow beat of Mrs. Morrison's heart. "She has a heartbeat."

"You're lying," Baker said.

Mays stepped back, removed the stethoscope, and handed it to Baker.

"Go ahead," she said, doing a dramatic wave toward Mrs. Morrison.

Baker pulled on a pair of latex gloves before seizing the stethoscope from Mays. He took a cautious step toward Mrs. Morrison.

"Don't worry, I don't bite," Mrs. Morrison said, grinning. The guards adjusted their guns, aligning red dots on her forehead, causing her to frown. "Can't you guys take a joke?"

Mays laughed.

Baker stiffened his back and made his last few steps bold. Stopping in front of Mrs. Morrison, he put on the stethoscope and checked her heartbeat.

"I'll be damned," he muttered, "she really does have a heartbeat."

"What?" one of the guards exclaimed.

"She has a heartbeat," Baker repeated.

"How is that possible?" The guard asked, then all eyes were on Mrs. Morrison.

"I don't know."

"Do you feel different now than before the bite?" Mays asked.

"I don't sleep anymore."

Mays cocked her head to the side, eyes boring into Mrs. Morrison's. "Why is that?"

"Deep down, I know that if I go to sleep, I won't wake up the same." Mrs. Morrison shrugged. "I won't be me anymore."

"So you willed away sleep," Mays said.

Mrs. Morrison nodded. "I guess so."

Baker shook his head in astonishment. "Remarkable. How do you remain alert? Don't you suffer from fatigue? Your cells..."

Mrs. Morrison shrugged. "I don't understand science-speak. I can't answer your questions with more than a *Sesame Street* vocabulary, so I figure your testing will help you better understand why I am still me."

"I noticed you sniffed the air while you were blindfolded ..." Mays stated.

"My sense of smell is heightened. What is mine has a unique scent. Joshua, Hope, and Sugar, my dog, are mine. Their scent seems to keep me calm. When they're too far from me, I get anxious and that anxiety turns into anger pretty fast."

Someone in the shadows used the word "imprinting." Mrs. Morrison knew what that was because she was a *Twilight* fanatic. Werewolves imprinted. Maybe all Reborns imprinted.

"Even if your children are not in danger?" Mays asked.

She nodded.

"Amazing," Mays commented. "Go on. What else have you noticed besides your improved hearing?"

"I can sense others like myself. It took some time for me to figure out that what I was feeling were Reborn."

Mays cocked her head to the side, regarding Mrs. Morrison. "What does it feel like?"

"It feels as if my skin is itching all over. I get a vibration, a weird buzz that makes my gums itch. It intensifies based on the proximity of the Reborn I sense."

She could tell Mays was ready to do a little jig of excitement, but being scientific, she kept it under control. "Is there anything else?"

Mrs. Morrison shook her head.

Mays knew better. "How about your appetite?"

"What?" Mrs. Morrison asked.

"You know what I'm talking about. Do you still eat regular human food or do you crave what your body lacks?"

"Like what?" Mrs. Morrison feigned ignorance.

"Considering your ischemic state, you would most likely crave blood, and when you entered a crisis, you would crave flesh like the others," Mays stated matter-of-factly.

"I can still eat regular food," Mrs. Morrison admitted reluctantly.

"Does it satisfy your appetite?" Mays questioned.

"Enough."

"Please elaborate."

"I do crave flesh—sometimes. It's triggered by the scent of blood," Mrs. Morrison began, her distaste for her new craving very apparent. "It started maybe two months after I was bitten. Me and the kids ran into a rabid pack of Reborn. There was a family being eaten alive. We couldn't help them." Mrs. Morrison shook her head, trying to rid herself of the memory of the family's screams. "No, I couldn't help them. So I did what I had to do to protect my kids, we got the hell out of there. It was hard for me to leave with the smell of blood in the air. It was intoxicating. I wanted to join the pack." Mrs. Morrison stared at her hands. "But I didn't. I protected my kids."

"Blood?"

"The scent of blood drew me." Mrs. Morrison shook her head against the memory. "I never wanted anything so bad."

"Did you bite the girl?" Mays asked.

"No! I didn't bite Hope. My husband and I found her in a house we were squatting in for the night. Her whole family had been slaughtered. The poor child was hiding in a closet under the stairs. If we didn't have Sugar, we would have never found her," Mrs. Morrison explained. "The child was so quiet."

"So she's not your daughter."

"I never said she was," Mrs. Morrison said, "but I've made her mine."

"What about the girl?" Mays asked.

"What about her?"

"Does the scent of blood agitate her? Can she eat regular food? Does she have a heightened sense of smell?" Mays pressed.

"No! Hope sleeps like any little girl her age that has been through a serious trauma, and that's barely. She manages to sleep only when I'm close by. Or Joshua or Sugar," she added. "She can't be by herself, and she does not tolerate strangers."

"So she's not like you?" Mays asked.

"I'm sure I said that already in plain English. Maybe I should try again in Spanish?"

"No," Mays held up her hands, "I believe you."

"But tests will confirm your claim," Baker chimed in.

Mays and Mrs. Morrison cut their eyes at Baker; only Mrs. Morrison's eyes glowed, and her lip curled before she growled. Baker quieted but made sure everyone could see his displeasure.

"No need to get upset, Mrs. Morrison. Sergeant Carter gave us a heads up a few days ago. He contacted a man in our group, Mr. Riggs, who relayed the information to us." Mays motioned to someone in the shadows. A girl in her early twenties stepped forward carrying what looked like an iPad. She had a stylus in her hand and was swirling it around on the face of the screen.

"Is Carter here? Is he en route?"

Sighing, Mays dropped her eyes and shook her head.

"I'm sorry, Mrs. Morrison, but we haven't heard from his team since he sent the message. I was told that it sounded like Carter and his team were being overrun by Reborn."

"Damn," Mrs. Morrison muttered.

"So Hope was bitten but is healing?" Mays inquired.

Mrs. Morrison nodded.

"The child couldn't have survived a bite," Baker said.

"Look, man, you're all about the complaints," Mrs. Morrison snarled. She was getting tired of his bitching and really wanted to hurt him. There was so much about the little man that she did not like but she had to play nice, for now. "How much do you actually know about Reborn?" Mrs. Morrison rolled her eyes. "I was going to take my family to Central Florida before I connected with Sergeant Carter. Was I stupid risking my kids' lives? Did Sergeant Carter lie about you guys and you're actually incompetent quacks?"

"I'll have you know that I hold a Ph.D. from both Harvard and MIT in genetics." Baker sniffed. "I am more than competent to handle your..." Baker waved his hand dismissively at Mrs. Morrison. "...condition."

"Enough, Baker." Mays raised the remote and aimed it at the screen again. This time all of the screens lit up. On them were a bunch of cells holding Reborns in various states. Mays used the remote as a pointer, starting with the screen on their left.

"You see that lethargic group?" Mays directed Mrs. Morrison's attention to a group of three Reborns. One of them paused then swayed from side to side before moving again.

"What's wrong with them." Mrs. Morrison stared at the screen. The Reborn reminded her of the one she put down with the dog leash.

"They are older, most likely senior citizens in their living days." Mays pressed buttons on the remote causing the image on the screen to zoom in. The Reborns' skin was gray and flakey. "Our tests show that the three on screen were in poor health and frail. Their health, or lack of health, seems to effect the density of their skin and bones in their new life."

"If you can call it life," Mrs. Morrison muttered.

Mays grinned, clicking a few buttons on the remote and restoring the image on the screen to its normal dimensions. She moved her remote to the next screen, again zooming in on the Reborns in the room. The room held about ten of them. They were all younger, children. Their ages had to be between five to their early teens. The Reborns moved naturally. Mrs. Morrison noticed that the younger ones kept running their hands along the furniture, walls, and at times the floor.

"Why are the little ones touching things?"

"We are not certain. They are still children, maybe it is a way of acquiring knowledge or an attempt to restore memory." Mays looked at Mrs. Morrison then back at the screen. "None of them speak."

"They're fast," a soldier said.

Mays nodded in agreement. "That they are. Their skin is a bit tougher than the seniors and the few adults we've managed to acquire."

"Are they intelligent?" Mrs. Morrison asked. Her memory conjured up the little Reborn that stalked them over a toy.

"Not that we can tell," Mays stated, her attention on the screen.

"Can you tell if they're growing?"

Mays shook her head. "We haven't had them long enough to find out."

"Where'd you get them?"

"That's classified."

Mrs. Morrison snorted. "Ah, the interesting stuff is always classified."

Mays laughed, it was a pretty sound. "What I can tell you is that men like the one outside are hard to kill. Their hides are tough, and if they were fighters in their conscious life, they are brutal in their second one."

Mrs. Morrison whistled. "I take it you guys have experienced them up close and personal-like."

Mays nodded. "We've lost some of our soldiers to the Morpheus Strain. We have been able to turn that loss into a benefit."

"You turn your soldiers into lab rats."

Mays shrugged. "It's only natural. We were able to document the course of the infection. The time it takes to take over the infected, as well as other things."

"The *other things* you mentioned are classified, right?"

"Correct," Mays confirmed. "It's a messy business, but it has led us to understanding the way the virus spreads."

"Speaking of mess, does anyone know how *this* mess started—the virus?" Mrs. Morrison asked Mays.

Mays held the bridge of her nose, squeezed, then looked Mrs. Morrison in the eyes. Both were back to their natural dark brown, Mays noted. "We believe Dr. Ivan Isaacs created the Morpheus Strain."

"Dr. who?" Mrs. Morrison cocked her head to the side.

"Only someone who knows genetics and virology could create a virus like the Morpheus Strain."

"The Morpheus Strain I know. I'm a carrier. Who's Isaacs?" Mrs. Morrison straightened, feeling a little fidgety.

"The fact that you don't know his name, we believe, is one of his motivations for creating the Morpheus Strain."

"That's a pretty desperate, if not, insane way to get attention." Mrs. Morrison folded her hands across her chest.

"Agreed, but nevertheless, there is nothing new under the sun. Dr. Isaacs did create the Morpheus Strain to put his name in lights, so to speak, but as we dug into his history, we found that Dr. Isaacs was terminally ill."

"You say was." Mrs. Morrison slid from the examination table. Red dots moved with her, never wavering from the center of her forehead.

Mays nodded. "Yes, like most of the population, cancer has no real cure. We have been able to coax it into remission, but there is never a guarantee that it will not return. As research has shown, when someone who has had cancer comes out of remission, the cancer that returns is more aggressive. Dr. Isaacs had pancreatic cancer. It seems the Morpheus rebooted his system, cured his cancer."

"Well, how did it cure him and mutate everyone else?"

"Dr. Isaacs' underlying intentions were motivated by self-preservation, but in truth he was—is—a brilliant scientist who wanted to help humanity."

"By making everyone sick," Mrs. Morrison said, unaware that her lip curled in disgust.

Mays shook her head. "Please bear with me a moment." Mays shoved her hands in her pockets. "As doctors and scientists, our goal is to do no harm. Our directive is to enhance life, not cripple it. We found out too late that Isaacs had added the Morpheus Strain in the formula of normal vaccinations. It was subtle. Isaacs' Morpheus Strain is difficult to detect. It has the ability to mimic the chemical properties of whatever vaccination it has been added to."

"So all these vaccinations that have been marketed to the public, as well as enforced by public schools, made everyone vulnerable to the Morpheus Strain."

Mays nodded.

"Goddamn him," Mrs. Morrison snarled.

"I believe Isaacs' intentions were not to make people sick but to rid the world of cancer and all other ailments," Mays explained.

"By exposing everyone."

"Yes." Mays nodded. "But he forgot one important factor."

"What's that?"

"We are all human beings but we're not the same. Our DNA makes us different. Something as simple as peanut butter can kill a small percentage of us, while many remain unaffected by it. It's the same with the Morpheus Strain. Some have dodged the bullet, so to speak, while others have literally died. It's man's uniqueness that Isaacs forgot."

Three shrill beeps drew everyone's attention to a digital clock above the door. Mrs. Morrison noticed the immediate change in the room. The guards resumed their positions, guns trained on her, while the doctors began pulling out needles, test tubes, labels, and Sharpies.

"Sorry about all the unpleasantness, Mrs. Morrison. Do you mind if I call you Esperanza?" Mays asked.

"Actually, I do."

"What would you prefer?"

"Mrs. Morrison."

"Oookaay." Mays did not hide her confusion.

"Look, my husband's name is all I have left of him," Mrs. Morrison stated.

"That's fine. It doesn't matter anyway." Mays pointed at the clock. "We only have an hour or so left in this place."

"What do you mean we only have an hour? Didn't Baker say that *we had all the time in the world?*"

Mays glared in Baker's direction. He had since slipped from the room. "Those of us who have remained uninfected are always mobile. We don't stay in one place too long."

"Why do that?" Mrs. Morrison inquired. "I mean, this place is like Fort Knox." Mrs. Morrison scanned the interior of the room. The walls were thick. Their technology still worked. They had electricity or damned powerful generators. Mrs. Morrison was sure they could last for at least another year or so, as long as they rationed supplies. It wasn't like life on the outside where stealth and movement were a matter of life and death.

"Well, Mrs. Morrison, it's because we suspect that Dr. Isaacs is alive and in hiding," Mays explained as she began pacing. "He infected everyone but managed to make himself immune, and for all we know, he may have made it so the Reborn will do *him* no harm."

"Well, he's a real charmer," Mrs. Morrison muttered.

"Agreed." Mays stopped pacing, turned, and then faced Mrs. Morrison. "No matter how poor of character Isaacs is, we have to stay off his radar until we can come up with a cure. If we don't, Isaacs is smart enough to undo any progress we make."

"Why would he do that?" Mrs. Morrison inquired.

"Oddly enough, he believes the Morpheus Strain is a success."

"How'd he come to that conclusion?"

Mays shrugged, along with several others in the room. "He may very well be insane. There's no way to tell for certain unless we confront the good doctor."

"I say you should just end him," Mrs. Morrison growled.

"Believe me, his death is part of our end game."

"Okay, how's he a threat?"

"Since he thinks a cure would undo all of his work, he is smart enough to update the Morpheus Strain to survive."

"What?"

"He can create a stronger strain by programming the virus to fight. At the moment, it is on the defensive. It evades cures, but it doesn't escalate to fatality."

Mrs. Morrison looked doubtful. "I guess that's a good thing."

Mays nodded.

"Do you at least have a plan to get this guy?"

"No. We need a way in ... a way to get close enough to Isaacs to not only kill him but destroy his research."

Mrs. Morrison nodded her head. "I see."

"Now that we have you, it looks like we have our in," Mays said, grinning.

"What do you mean?"

"Being that Dr. Isaacs is obsessed with the idea of immortality, when he finds out about you and Hope, he is going to want to acquire you."

"You plan to use me and Hope as bait?" Mrs. Morrison backed away from Mays.

Mays ignored Mrs. Morrison's discomfort. "Isaacs doesn't want to die. He realizes that his plan failed, but you and Hope are the key to immortality."

"What?" Mrs. Morrison asked, leaning against an examination table.

"Isaacs has been studying the Reborn. We've tagged a few, released them so we could monitor their movements, possibly document habits. Some of our tagged specimens have disappeared."

"They could have just stopped moving. That can happen, right?" Mrs. Morrison's eyes were drawn to the elderly Reborn. The one that had stopped earlier was again standing still, very still. There was no swaying.

Mays shrugged. "We're not sure. We have found carcasses that have been dismembered."

"That could be a human thing. You've heard of morbid curiosity," Mrs. Morrison stated matter-of-factly.

"Of course, but the way the carcasses are dismembered have the tell-tale signature of surgical prowess.

Some carcasses would be missing various organs, while others were diseased."

"How can the dead be sick?" one of the guards chimed in.

"Because the majority of the population is not dead," Mays replied. "I don't think people are truly dead but sick." She tapped a well-manicured nail on the desk she leaned on. "I believe the Morpheus Strain caused an ischemic event."

"Ischemic?" Mrs. Morrison said, her confusion written all over her face. "You've used that word before and I don't know what it means."

"Ischemia." Mays shook her head. "Sorry for assuming you understood the terminology. I've been surrounded by medical and scientific personnel for so long, I just—forget it. Ischemia is a restriction of the blood supply to living tissue. This restriction reduces much-needed oxygen and glucose that the cells need to metabolize, or survive. It seems the bites trigger a mutated form of ischemia."

"Which causes the body to start shutting down on a cellular level," Mrs. Morrison said.

Mays nodded. "Yes, but when the virus was designed, it failed in the rebooting."

Cocking her head to the side, Mrs. Morrison regarded her in bewilderment. "What do you mean?"

"The goal for its creator was to reprogram the body to maximum health, like rebooting a computer after an update. It's not until the system shuts down that all the old gets pushed out of the system. Turning it on allows new coding to overwrite the faulty scripting."

"So those who were bitten, like myself, are plain old doomed?"

"No, Mrs. Morrison. You are salvageable, like I am certain many of the infected are."

"Huh? I'm not a zombie?"

Mays laughed. It was a nice sound, like the tinkling of bells. "*Zombie* is such a Hollywood term. Besides, they don't exist."

"Well, what are all those things walking around outside?" Mrs. Morrison questioned.

"Ischemics."

"Ischemics? I think I like zombies better."

"What?" Mays planted her hands on her hips.

"It sounds less nerdy."

"None of that matters. The facts are, most of the infected walking around outside can be salvaged. For instance, you are not truly dead, but more or less half-dead." Mays cocked her head to the right, her eyes traveling down Mrs. Morrison's body. "I mean, your skin has a mild gray tint to it, but it hasn't cracked like most. Your mobility is not lethargic. You have full mental capacity." Mays tapped her head.

Mays snapped her fingers. "Oh, I can't forget the heartbeat. I mean, you're the first ever to have a heartbeat."

Mrs. Morrison narrowed her eyes. "What do you mean by the first ever?"

"As you've noticed on the screen, we have collected Reborn for control groups."

"What happens with these control groups?" Mrs. Morrison asked, getting the feeling that things were about to go south.

"Don't worry about it. You will never be dissected for study."

"What are you going to do?"

"Take blood samples, of course," Mays replied. "We need to see what makes your genetics so unique that you are resistant to the virus. Also, we need to inject you with nanites."

"Nanites?"

"Yes." Mays said. "Don't worry. These nanites are for research purposes. They are preprogrammed to troubleshoot your system. They enter via your bloodstream and record your medical stats. Those stats are transmitted to a satellite relay, where the data is stored in a cloud that is only accessible to members of our research team."

When Mrs. Morrison held up her hands, three targets overlapped at the center of her forehead.

"Give it a rest, boys," Mays snapped.

"I thought human experimentation was taboo."

"Of course it was when we had a functional government which regulated medical research. Since our government fractured, us scientific types have been allowed to set aside scruples and do whatever it takes to salvage what's left of humanity."

Mrs. Morrison shook her head in disgust. "What happened to do no harm?"

"You can't make an omelet if you don't crack a few eggs. The eggs we crack are so far gone that they can no longer be classified as human."

"You're sounding a bit like Isaacs."

"No, we're being practical," Mays stated. "Seeing that time is of the essence, we don't really have time to be hindered too heavily by morals. Besides, we're only using the sick. We are testing cures on them. If they get better, that means we are on to something. If they don't," Mays shrugged, "it's back to the drawing board."

"That's pretty gangsta." Mrs. Morrison said.

"Gangster indeed," Mays said, grinning. "But necessary."

"What else do these nanites do?" Mrs. Morrison's intuition warned her that the nanites' purpose was not completely to her benefit.

"Several will break off and attach to your heart and brain, so if you find yourself shutting down, we can stop you from attacking the team you will be working with."

Mrs. Morrison didn't like the idea of being tagged, but she could understand the logic. She wasn't sure how long her mind would remain *hers*, so it would be best for everyone if she had a fail-safe installed. She would have to find a way to tell Joshua and Hope.

"I'll do it," Mrs. Morrison stated.

"It's not like you had a choice," Baker muttered.

Mays glared at him. "I think you should go, Baker."

Baker didn't move. He glared at Mrs. Morrison, who looked very bored. "Look, Baker, if you want to see who is the man in this relationship," Mrs. Morrison took a bold step forward. Not a gun in the room lifted. "We can work this out right here, right now."

Mays placed a staying hand on Mrs. Morrison's arm and shook her head.

"Leave," Mays ground out.

Baker trembled with rage, but he spun on his heel and exited the room and crashed into someone. A box hit the floor, something shattered, and a vigorous stream of profanities followed accented by Baker's utterance, "Well, *you* should watch where you're going."

Chapter 3

HOPE

1010 Hours - En Route to Juvenile Holding Area

Hope looked sideways at the unpleasant man in the starched white shirt, vest, and dress slacks. The man, Baker, purposely walked fast, pulling her along behind him. His fingers bit into her skin, just above the area where he let the Reborn bite her. It hurt. There was a sick fascination in his mud-brown eyes when she cried. He'd laughed at her. He'd even told her that he'd see if she really had *miracle blood.*

Hope wanted to scream at him...bite him and make him hurt like he'd hurt her. The problem with Hope was that she had lost her words a long time ago, when her mother, Veronica Walls, shoved her in a closet and told her to be quiet or the monsters would get her. The Reborn that broke into her home and took away her little brothers...even the baby, and finally her parents, stole her voice. So many times she wanted to burst from the closet and help her parents, but her mom's tears and the promise she made Hope make forced her to stay put.

"You're all we've got left, baby girl." Veronica wept. "You have to survive."

"But mama, I can help. I'll fight." Hope declared. "I don't wanna be alone."

Veronica shook her head, took Hope's hand, and placed it over her heart. Hope frowned at the speed at which her mother's heart beat. "Baby, me, and your daddy, even your brothers survive if you do. You're all this family has left." Veronica raised Hope's hand to her lips and kissed it. It was at that moment, Hope believed her mother had done something magical. A mother's kiss healed all ills and Hope supposed that if she kept her promise, nothing would ever hurt her again. The few times Hope's family had gone to church, the pastor always declared that family watched over family even in the afterlife. Hope embraced that.

Her father screamed. Hope jumped. Her mother shoved her deeper into the closet, rose, then stepped away. "Promise me you'll live."

Hope looked in her mother's eyes and nodded. Her mother stepped away, closed the door, and died. Hope heard every second of it. Her words died that day too.

Hope sat quietly in the closet for a long time while Reborn shuffled around outside. A few times, they beat on the closet door, but Hope retreated deep inside herself to a quiet place. A place where she was safe. Hope got tired after a while, so tired that she thought she would break her promise to her mom. So she asked her mom to help her, and that's when Mr. and Mrs. Morrison, Joshua, and Sugar came. They saved her.

The man shook her. Hope glared at him.

"Are you going to bite me?" Baker sneered.

Hope's eyes became slits. She took in her surroundings, noting that the corridors had numbers painted on the walls near the ceiling. The paint was luminous. The man shook her again.

"Pay attention." Baker hissed, he'd leaned down so he was close to Hope's ear. Hope saw a soldier look in their direction. The soldier, Kidd, frowned then started moving in their direction.

"Look, girl," Baker spoke her gender as if it offended him. "You will say nothing to the soldiers, your mother, or Mays about our little trip." Baker's hand slid up Hope's arm and squeezed the bandaged bite that was hidden under her shirt.

Hope glared at him.

"I'll know if you tell." Hope's eyes widened. "I know a little something about Reborn. I treated the bite so your mother can't smell it." Baker's mouth curved in a nasty smile. "She won't see it. No one will see the bite. Besides, you need our protection," Baker continued, as Kidd drew closer. "The boy and your dog are of no value to us. They can be left behind at any time."

Hope paled. It became hard for her to breathe.

"I promise you, if you cooperate, I'll make sure nothing happens to the boy and the dog."

Kidd was only six feet away from them.

Baker squeezed her arm tighter, making her wince. Kidd's steps quickened.

"Are we in agreement?" Baker whispered.

Hope nodded.

"What are you doin' to the girl, Baker?"

Baker released Hope, who moved to stand behind Kidd. Baker did not acknowledge Kidd.

"Look, Baker." Kidd stepped into Baker's personal space, backing him into a wall while the other soldiers looked away. "I know you think you're somebody." Kidd lifted his finger and pointed it squarely between Baker's eyes. "The world may not be what it used to be, but I'll be damned if I stand around and let you bully a child."

"I'm your superior."

Several of the soldiers laughed at Baker's declaration.

"You ain't nothin' but a stuffed shirt." Kidd took a step back, looking Baker up and down. "This little girl," Kidd pointed in Hope's direction. "She may very well save everyone's life."

Baker sniffed at Kidd's statement.

Kidd shoved Baker against the wall, smiling when the man's head audibly connected with the wall. "You will treat that little girl like she's the Holy Grail."

Kidd released Baker, who rubbed his head, straightened his shirt, and then tugged on his lab coat before extending his attention to Kidd.

"You will bring the children and their animal to the examination room." Baker put some space between the irate soldier and himself.

Kidd glared at Baker. Baker stood his ground.

"Kidd." Another soldier had joined them. "He ain't worth it."

Kidd broke eye contact with Baker. "He a dick."

"You get no argument out of me on that," the soldier said.

Baker turned a bored look on Kidd and his companion. "Mays expects the children to be delivered to the examination immediately."

"Sure," the soldier agreed, clapping a hand on Kidd's shoulder and pulling him away from Baker.

Baker turned his back and walked away. They would be leaving the facility soon and he had much to do.

Mays thought she was the lead researcher. Baker laughed to himself. He would show her. If the girl was what the monster said she was, then *he* would be the one to engineer a cure.

Chapter 4

1050 HOURS - EXAMINATION Room

A tall African American man wearing a Chicago Police Department uniform stepped forward. He had his hands clasped behind his back, military style. His hair was cut close to the scalp. His onyx eyes studied her. Mrs. Morrison could tell he wasn't too keen on her ability to breathe.

"My name is Travis Riggs. Most folks call me Trigga."

"That's nice." Mrs. Morrison gasped at yet another needle piercing her skin. She wasn't afraid of needles but she was really starting to hate them.

"I will be the lead on Caravan 1. You," Travis pointed at Mrs. Morrison, "your children, and the doc here, are my cargo. I am the team's alpha which means I'm everyone's boss."

The click of a door opening drew everyone's attention. Hope walked in carrying Joshua in her arms. Sugar was right behind her. Baker followed. He made brief eye contact with Mrs. Morrison's before joining the others in the shadows. Mays stepped back, allowing Mrs. Morrison the necessary room to gather up her sleeping son. She then helped Hope onto the examination table, noticing the brief pained expression on her face when she pulled Hope's her arm. Sugar lay under the examination table. Once everyone settled, Mays moved in to continue administering shots and record Mrs. Morrison's vitals.

Trigga cleared his throat then folded his impressive arms across his chest. All activity within the room ceased. "In about forty-five minutes, four caravans will exit this facility. These caravans will contain three vehicles each: one armored vehicle, one all terrain vehicle, and an RV." Trigga began pacing. "One of the caravan units is a decoy that will, if the team survives, serve as a rear guard for the convoy closest to them."

Mrs. Morrison exhaled, her heart rate quickened slightly.

"Each caravan unit has a set mission and destination." Trigga stopped pacing, faced the group, eyes locked with Mrs. Morrison's. "It's my job to guard the VIPs." He broke eye contact and turned his gaze on the people in the room. "It's all of our jobs to get this world, at least what's left of it, up and running again."

The soldiers in the room, saluted, moving into a fully attentive stance.

"There are already some established checkpoints on every route. We have campsites and provisions in various locations. Each team has a satellite phone. Some have more and since power will be an issue once we leave this facility, we have specific times in which we communicate. Other than that, we only use those phones in a dire emergency. "

He paused again, his gaze doing a second rotation around the room. No one moved, a few people audibly swallowed.

"There has been an established set of code words so each team can recognize friendlies."

"But what if the friendlies are compromised?" Mrs. Morrison interjected. She knew he was psyching the men up. It was standard for athletes and military before a big game or battle. They were all about to jump into the thick of things.

"What will be, will be." Trigga said with some venom. "This world ain't what it was and we," his arm did a slow rotation of the room, "have been living in the lap of luxury for a little over a year and things are about to get real."

He paused, making eye contact with all the soldiers in the room. "Are you up for the challenge?"

"Sir! Yes sir!"

Trigga grinned, cupping his hand over his ear, leaning in a little. "I'm sorry children, I didn't hear you."

"Sir! Yes sir!" The soldiers shouted then drew into battle stance.

Trigga smiled, bobbing his head to a phantom beat. "That's what I like to hear." He dismissed the men then stationed himself several feet away from the examination table. Sugar growled at him. He growled back.

"Mr. Riggs." May's soft accented voice silenced the growls.

Trigga pulled into a military stance and ignored Mrs. Morrison and her family. Mays turned to Mrs. Morrison with a large needle in her hand.

"This is the last one," Mays slid the needle under Mrs. Morrison's skin. She distracted herself with the bundle in her arms. Joshua was still asleep. She stroked his hair, his face, and bent to kiss his brow.

"Do you mind my asking a question about your son?" Mays withdrew the needle, bagged it, and then discarded it.

"What do you want to know?" Mrs. Morrison said without taking her eyes off of Joshua. Hope had her arms wrapped around Mrs. Morrison's waist with her head pressed into Mrs. Morrison's back.

"Did you find him, like you found Hope?" Mays asked.

Mrs. Morrison shook her head. "No, he is my son."

"Adopted?"

Mrs. Morrison nodded.

"How long have you had him?

"Why do you ask?"

"The child's distress over seeing your husband," Mays began, "—may be problematic."

Mrs. Morrison cupped Joshua's chin. "All of us are going to be problematic if Grant managed to survive." She smiled wanly.

"How so?"

"Grant's the love of my life, but for Josh, he's the only father he knows. Besides, he follows us." Mrs. Morrison's smile gained strength as she recollected helping Joshua root through a clearance rack in Walmart for a Father's Day shirt for Grant. They found one. It was way too small, powder blue, and cutesy, but they took it anyway. Grant was into power clothes and colors, but he instantly loved anything Joshua gave him.

Mrs. Morrison's smile grew as she recalled Joshua's presentation of the shirt to his father, how his little face fell when Grant accepted it and promptly ripped it. Joshua almost cried, but Grant being Grant, made the strips of shirt honorable. He declared to Joshua that he would wear his gift like a badge of honor, then explained to Joshua the meaning of armbands to military personnel. He then showed Joshua the most important words on his shirt, "World's Greatest Dad." Grant and Joshua made a ceremony of tying the strip of shirt around Grant's arm, making sure to keep the word Dad visible. Grant declared it his tribute to Joshua. Joshua's little chest puffed with pride and she fell deeper in love with him.

"He follows you?"

"Yes. He has since he was turned."

Mays looked to Trigga who responded "Not a problem."

Nodding, Mays picked up her iPad and began studying the screen. "Well, I am finished."

"What happens now?" Mrs. Morrison's eyes never left her son's face.

"You and your family will go with Mr. Riggs and his team."

"Where are we going?" Mrs. Morrison finally gave Mays her full attention.

Mays glanced at Trigga who nodded.

"We will be going to the Johnson Space Center."

"A space station?" Mrs. Morrison asked.

Mays nodded.

"Why?"

"The space center has a fully functional lab. We need the proper equipment to engineer a cure. It's one of the few secure facilities standing."

"How so?" Mrs. Morrison's gaze returned to her sleeping boy.

"Reinforced walls and doors. Also, it is connected to satellites that allow us Internet access, which is impossible anywhere else," Mays explained.

"I'll be damned. Google lives." Mrs. Morrison beamed then her expression sobered. "Once a cure had been produced, what then?"

"We have scientists working on a universal delivery method. The details they have not shared with us, I am assuming because it has not been perfected."

"Hmm."

"Mama," Joshua murmured, his voice scratchy. He opened his left eye, stretched, and then opened his right eye.

"Yes, baby?"

"Is Daddy comin' with us?" Joshua was still a little groggy but his eyes were alight with hope.

Mays and Mrs. Morrison shared a look then Mrs. Morrison spoke. "I told you before, baby, Daddy can't come with us because he's sick."

"I know, but he'll come anyway. He loves us."

Mrs. Morrison groaned. How could she explain it so he would understand? Just as she opened her mouth, a blaring alarm went off.

A map of the facility popped up on the screen over the entry door. There were a lot of moving green dots and one red one. The red one was causing the green dots to disappear.

"What's going on?" Joshua asked drowsily.

"I don't know, baby," Mrs. Morrison replied, looking to Mays for answers. Suddenly, her skin began to itch, along with her gums. Reborn!

"We have a breach," Trigga stated, as he walked toward the screen. He pointed at the dots. "The green dots are our people. The red dot is an intruder."

"Grant," Mrs. Morrison whispered.

Everyone looked at her.

"How do you know?"

"I told you, I can sense what is mine. Grant is my husband. I love him. Never stopped even after he was bitten. It's not like I had a choice in leaving him. Fate sort of forced my hand."

A smiling Joshua squirmed in her arms.

"I've been running, not because I want to. I have to." Mrs. Morrison glanced at the door. "Maybe that's why I don't feel him like I used to," she muttered to herself. "He feels like one of them now."

"Daddy would never hurt us," Joshua rasped.

"Baby, we can't be sure of that because he's sick." Mrs. Morrison shook her head and Joshua frowned. "So he can't come with us."

"When we make him better?" Joshua tried again.

"Of course, baby," she lied, then kissed Joshua on the forehead and handed him over to Mays.

Mrs. Morrison placed her hands over Hope's. "Listen, baby girl, I have to go talk to Grant."

Hope removed her hands from Mrs. Morrison's waist and sat upright.

"I need you to go with Mr. Riggs here." Mrs. Morrison pointed at Trigga.

Hope nodded.

After helping Hope off the examination table, Mrs. Morrison kissed her on the forehead, slid from the table, then put her fist to her chest, and tapped it three times.

Hope hugged Mrs. Morrison tight then moved away.

Mrs. Morrison pointed at Sugar. "What about you?"

Sugar barked.

"Good girl." Mrs. Morrison knelt down so she could take a good-bye kiss from Sugar.

"You don't have to confr—" Mrs. Morrison gave a quick shake of her head before Mays finished her sentence.

"I mean, we don't need you to talk to your husband."

"Yes you do," Mrs. Morrison stated. "If I don't, he's going to mess up your evacuation plan."

"He can't possibly," exclaimed an incredulous Baker as he entered the room.

"Look, you guys are the ones that showed me the different types of Reborn and Grant is the hard to kill kind. He's fit. He was healthy before he became one of them and he's still got his skills from his days as an Army Ranger."

"Still, he can't stop us from leaving." Mays waved her arm at the heavily armed soldiers in the room.

"Look, I can make him stop." Mrs. Morrison pointed at the screen and the big red dot that was heading their way. "You need him to slow down. I can give you guys time to get yourselves situated."

Mays grabbed Mrs. Morrison's shoulder. "You're too valuable for us to risk."

Mrs. Morrison looked up at the screen of rapidly vanishing green dots. "Look, I'm not doing this for you." Mrs. Morrison glanced over at a fully alert and smiling Joshua. "I need to handle this."

"Emergency Protocol Initiated" A digital female voice burst from the speakers.

"He's hit one of the generators," Baker exclaimed.

Mrs. Morrison walked over to Trigga. "Take care of my kids."

Trigga nodded.

"I need my things." Mrs. Morrison held out her hand.

Trigga looked over her shoulder to Mays, who held up the iPad, waved it and nodded.

Trigga just stared at her like she'd called him a nasty name.

"Its okay, Mr. Riggs." Mays waved the iPad again. "Let her go."

Trigga took a deep breath. "Once you exit this room from that door, you're going to head left and follow the screams," Mays replied, just as screaming began not too far from where they were.

Mrs. Morrison nodded then turned to leave.

"Wait." It was Riggs who spoke.

Mrs. Morrison faced him. He tossed Maxine, her baton, and a small square to her. She automatically caught each item and slid them in their proper holders. She eyeballed the map then looked up at Trigga.

"What's this?"

"A map to where we'll be waiting for you," Trigga told her.

The alarm switched to a digital feminine voice. "Initiating countdown."

"This place goes boom in about 20 minutes," Trigga said. "It gives everyone who can make it a chance to get to their perspective exit points. We can wait for you at least five minutes prior to detonation. If you don't make it—well..."

"Understood," Mrs. Morrison replied, then sprinted through the door one of the guards opened for her which she quickly exited.

Mays and Trigga watched her on the screen. The kid, Joshua kept squirming in his arms. He put him down, dropped to his knee, and made sure to make eye contact. "Look, I need you to stand over there with your sister." Hope was sitting against a wall toward the back of the room, there was a door beside her, and it was hard to see in the shadows. She stroked Sugar's head. Joshua moved in Hope's direction. Satisfied, Trigga turned toward the video screen.

"You sure that was a good idea doc?"

Mays nodded. "She's been tagged."

"What's that got to do with anything?"

"The nanites allow us to track her but they also build in her a need to return home." Mays tapped the screen of her iPad.

Trigga nodded, not quite clear on what was going on, but he trusted the doc. Mays was nice to her, more of a good cop thing. Morrison needed to feel like there was an ally among them. It made their job easier. A cooperative prisoner who believed they were free was easy to transport. What was even better was the fact that Morrison would fight for them as well."

Trigga stepped away from Mays and began barking orders to his people. None of them noticing Joshua slip away.

Chapter 5

HEarT TO HEarT

1127 Hours — Basement Corridors

Lights flickered and failed by the time Mrs. Morrison got five feet away from the examination room. The wash of red emergency lights flooded the rounded space. Exposed piping made her feel like she was literally walking down someone's throat. She nearly choked on the palpable odor of fear, urine and feces as she began to move against the fleeing mass.

A man stumbled into her, placing his meaty palm in the center of her chest just over her breasts. Her hand lifted, curled into a fist and drew back like a bow being knocked in for firing, but she froze when the man yanked his hand away, muttered an embarrassed apology before stumbling off. She looked around at several others, their eyes stretched wide as they struggled through the darkened halls. For her, everything was as clear.

Night vision.

She forgot to disclose that.

Bones cracked. Mrs. Morrison's head snapped in the direction of the disturbance. Copper. She smelled the copper which pulled her into a jog. There was something about it that ignited the hunger in her feral side—the diseased part. But for some reason, the craving wasn't kicking in like it had a few times before, particularly the first two months after being bitten.

The first time, Josh scraped his knee, normal childish clumsiness forced her to walk away from him. The second was after a rabid Reborn bit Hope. After the adrenaline from fighting off the bastard, Mrs. Morrison's own cravings turned her into a threat driving her to take a brief walkabout, leaving Sugar to keep watch over her children while she wrestled for control. Control became second nature when it came to her kids. Being away from them was like lemon juice on a paper cut. She worried for their safety. Sugar would defend them to the death, but if Sugar fell who would keep them safe? Safety. Her need for her kids to be safe kept Mrs. Morrison's humanity in place.

Her boot slid in a puddle. She stopped, looked down and grimaced. Blood. A pool of it formed an awkward circle around her booted foot. She looked up as she righted herself noticing several more, all leading to the end of the corridor. It split in two directions, left or right. The left corner was partially collapsed making the right an obvious choice. Taking a deep breath, Mrs. Morrison squared her shoulders, exhaled then followed the trail of blood.

A ragged rasping breath made her aware of the absence of fleeing footfalls. The quiet unsettled her. Her footsteps bounced off the walls creating an eerie melody drawing her heart to join in, beating rapidly. She hadn't seen Grant up close since he was bitten. He kept his distance and she was grateful for that, but what had he become. Did he eat flesh like the others? Did he feel Hope and Josh like she could? Did he feel her? Was that how he tracked them? Why couldn't she feel him anymore? Her head hurt as more questions flooded her mind, ending with the most troubling one, *Why couldn't she feel him anymore*, she wondered, as she stopped at the edge of the corridor.

"Fffaaammiillleeee," Grant rasped.

Someone whimpered and the smell of urine surged, cutting through dust, moisture and rust.

Mrs. Morrison took another deep breath, her heartbeat quickened then resumed its normal slow tempo before she turned the corner to face Grant.

Grant was growling at Kidd, a private, probably a new recruit from the way he trembled. His chocolate brown eyes were wide. They seemed to stretch even wider when they settled on her.

Mrs. Morrison frowned. She wanted to shake her head with compassion as she noticed his soiled uniform. She schooled her expression, keeping it passive, shifting her eyes to Grant, who was standing in front of Kidd.

"Baby," Mrs. Morrison murmured.

Grant's head snapped up. He tossed Kidd, not caring where he fell then turned to face her.

Kidd ended up a few feet away, setting him in the middle of the corridor where he had a clear path to the examination room she'd left. Kidd struggled to rise and succeeded, though unsteady. His frightened gaze darting between her and Grant, then settled on her.

'Go,' she mouthed. Kidd scrambled away from them, limping, but moving.

"Baby," she tried again.

Grant didn't move but his eyes devoured her. There were chunks of flesh missing from his right cheek. Dents marred his black body armor from shoulder to chest. A particularly deep dent rested over his heart.

"Faaammiillee," Grant rasped.

"That's right, baby. I'm family." She didn't budge.

Grant nodded.

"You have to stop this."

"Protect family," Grant declared.

"We're not in danger, baby." Mrs. Morrison wanted to go to him so bad. If he held her as he was now, would it be the same?

Grant beat his chest. "Protect family," he declared again.

"You're hurting people who mean us no harm."

"Ffaaammiillee," Grant whispered, pointed at her, and then placed his hand on his chest, over his heart.

"We have to go," Mrs. Morrison told him. "And you have to let us."

Grant said nothing. He moved toward her. She didn't budge.

Mrs. Morrison looked down, hooking her locket with her index finger. Her eyes burned. Maybe she could still shed real tears.

Grant placed his hand over hers. His free one, the right one, rested on her shoulder. It was wet. His finger slide along her collarbone leaving a trail of blood which ended at the apex of her locket. His hands were a blend of grayish marble and pale flesh. A muted electric blue light seeped through the cracks in Grant's skin. Mrs. Morrison sighed, let her locket go then wrapped her hand around Grant's. He let her move it. She pushed it away, lifting it high enough to rest her cheek against it. All she wanted was to fall into his arms and for everything else to be a bad dream. If only she could get a do-over for her life—*their life*. She wanted their home back. She wanted their family back, just like Grant did, but they couldn't be like that anymore. They couldn't be a family. She released his hand, which drifted slowly down and hung loosely at his side.

"Baby, no." She took hold of the hand that had drifted back to her shoulder and pulled.

Grant's grip tightened.

"No." He ran his finger along the spot where he had bitten her. "Family. Family is together," he whispered, drawing her to him.

"You're sick, baby." She shook her head. "We can't."

"No," Grant growled, his grip tightened.

"Daddy?"

Mrs. Morrison stopped breathing.

"Jooossshhheee," Grant bellowed.

Mrs. Morrison turned. There was Joshua, in the middle of all that blood. He should have been traumatized by the pile of bodies along the walls, but all Joshua saw was his daddy. It was in his devout gaze.

"Daddy," Joshua said again, taking a step toward them.

"Joshua, go back to Mr. Riggs!"

"No!" Joshua screamed. His steps quickened.

Grant's grip loosened on her shoulder, which was all she needed. Mrs. Morrison kneed him in the right hipbone. Grant doubled over.

Good. He could still feel pain, she thought as she slid from his grasp. She pulled her baton from its sheath and kneecapped him as she regained her footing. But unlike the old woman, Grant's bones were very strong. She heard something crack, but it wasn't Grant's bones, it was something in her baton.

Damn it! She needed to slow him down so she could get Joshua away from him.

What the hell? She thought as she pulled back her arm. She just needed her fist to be strong enough to break his kneecap. She let go, putting all she had in her punch. Mrs. Morrison heard her skin tear, felt it harden, as her fist descended. This time, the cracking sound was Grant's kneecap.

"Daddy!" Joshua shouted.

Mrs. Morrison moved but Grant grabbed her shoulder as he fell. She twisted around, opened her mouth, and bit Grant on the forearm. He let her go and she ran, scooping up a screaming Joshua along the way. She reached into her back pocket, pulled out the map and shook it open without missing a step. She would have to stop to read it. She didn't want to do that but she slowed her pace.

The map, though it looked like plain paper, was actually digital. A flashing blue light pulsed, the name of the corridor, or rather the number, Corridor Four, blinked over it. Several clicks away from the blue spot was a big flashing yellow X, which she concluded was the rendezvous point.

Mrs. Morrison stopped, tightened her grip on Joshua, who was screaming at the top of his lungs, "I want daddy! I want daddy!" She scanned the corridor, comparing it to the map. Sure enough, Corridor Four was high on her right.

"Jooossshheee!" Grant wailed.

Joshua screamed even louder.

"Sorry, kiddo," Mrs. Morrison said, as she took off down the corridor. She almost passed the small tunnel which led to the docking area. Joshua kicked and screamed all the way.

Grant's footsteps thundered in the distance as Joshua's screams escalated. Her gaze flicked from the tunnel to the corridor Grant would emerge through, then down to her wailing son. She had to get him to be still so they could get through quickly.

"Sorry, champ," Mrs. Morrison whispered then hit him. Joshua's screams stopped abruptly. He was limp in her arms. She used just enough force to knock him out. It was the first time she ever hit Joshua. It made her feel dirty.

"Six minutes to detonation." A digitized feminine voice filled the corridors.

Mrs. Morrison packed away her feelings, adjusted Joshua's small body so they could get through the tunnel. He would hurt, but Joshua left her no choice. His screams amplified Grant's protective instinct which was what probably drove him into a primal state, Mrs. Morrison thought as she considered the amount of bodies that littered the corridor they'd fled through.

The convoy was probably gone already, but maybe she and Joshua could get clear of the blast.

Mrs. Morrison increased her speed when she noticed the light at the end of the tunnel.

"Detonation in four minutes."

Smelling fresh air, she pushed hard, pulling Joshua closer, tightening her grip. She cleared the tunnel as the computerized voice announced three minutes.

"Morrison!" Trigga shouted. He leaned off the tail end of a Toyota FJ Cruiser.

She ran just as the driver kicked the car into gear.

The first explosion hit, shaking the ground causing Mrs. Morrison to nearly drop to her knees. She pushed forward, latching on to the Toyota's bumper with her left hand as she held Josh tight with the other. She kept up with the fleeing vehicle, pulling herself close enough to hand Joshua over to a wide-eyed

Trigga, who took him. She pushed herself up, scrambling up the side. She grabbed onto the roof rack then pulled herself up. The FJ Cruiser didn't slow but kept moving.

Mrs. Morrison glanced to the left in time to see an old Land Cruiser drive away from them. When she looked right, there a black Chevy Tahoe equipped with bull bars. It sped off in the opposite direction. She wondered where they were headed.

"Where's Hope and Sugar?" She shouted over the noise of the explosion.

Trigga jerked his head toward the back seat. Sugar poked her head out of the back window and barked while wagging her tail furiously. Hope had Sugar by the neck. Her eyes, like always, were trained on her, taking note of her expressions and body language.

Mays sat in the front passenger seat. She was holding an iPad that was in a yellow military grade case with dark gray rubber backing. It had a strap that Mays slipped her hand through. When they were far enough away, the driver stopped. Trigga passed Josh to Mrs. Morrison as everyone turned to watch the fireworks. He climbed up to join her.

"What happened to the kid?" Trigga's usual hard mask softened as he took in Joshua's unconscious form, frowning when he noticed the bruise.

"He saw his father."

"Damn." He placed a hand on Joshua's face, letting his large finger slide across his cheek, stopping at the bruise.

"I don't think he's going to like me too much when he comes to."

"Why's that?"

Mrs. Morrison's gaze settled on Trigga's fingers. "I did that." Her grip tightened on her son. "I had to."

Trigga's hand fell from Joshua's face.

"He saw me fight Grant." She swallowed then licked her lips before she continued. "I left Grant behind."

She looked at Trigga as fresh tears fell from the corner of her eyes. "I killed my husband and I hurt my son."

"I know you did it to save him." Trigga placed his large hands on her shoulders. "You're more human than most of the people I've met since this mess happened." He squeezed her shoulders. "He'll forgive you."

"I hope so," she whispered.

"He will, you're his mom."

"Hmm," Mays murmured, then tapped the iPad's screen.

"What's up, Doc?" Trigga inquired, hopping down from the Cruiser to move over to her side of the vehicle.

Mays frowned at the screen. "I guess it's nothing."

"What do you mean?" Trigga leaned into the passenger window so he could see the screen.

"Well, you know how Mrs. Morrison's signature is blue because of the nanites in her bloodstream." Mays tapped the screen showing Mrs. Morrison's signature. "Well, I could have sworn I saw one pop up when the building started going down."

"What?" Trigga leaned in farther to see the screen better.

"You can stop looking. It's gone now." Mays was still staring at the screen.

"Well it seems to have you spooked."

"No. It was a glitch that's all," Mays said, finally looking away from the device. She turned around in her seat. "Do we have everyone?"

"Yeah," Trigga replied. "We'll be meeting up with the rest of my team at sunset."

Mays settled into her seat. "Good."

"Get in, Morrison," Trigga opened the door for her.

She passed Joshua to Hope, who she set him between herself and Sugar. Mrs. Morrison slid in, followed by Trigga who closed the door.

The driver was Baker of all people. He frowned at her via the rearview mirror then set his eyes ahead.

Mrs. Morrison understood that she and Baker would never be besties. She would probably kill him if the opportunity presented itself. He gave her the creeps, especially when she caught him staring at Hope, but for now, she would have to tolerate him.

The FJ Cruiser began to move. Mrs. Morrison settled in for the drive, reaching for her locket, gasping when her searching fingers found nothing.

"Crap!" Mrs. Morrison exclaimed. The truck stopped. Everyone turned to look at her.

"What?" Trigga, Baker, and Mays asked.

"Nothing." Mrs. Morrison let her fingers slide down her naked throat.

"What is it with you women and the word nothing." Trigga threw his hands up, letting them fall with a slap into this lap.

"It's nothing really. I lost a locket back there, probably when I was getting away from Grant."

"It's just jewelry," Trigga said.

Mrs. Morrison nodded.

Trigga gazed out his window.

It wasn't just a piece of jewelry. It was, besides her last name, the last piece of Grant's humanity. A reminder of who he was before—what they were before.

Mrs. Morrison looked out at the old River North Theater. They were on their way to Lake Shore Drive. She figured they would take that route and hit the highway to get to wherever they were going. She sighed. All she had were her memories. What worried her about that was they depended on how long she kept her humanity, which was an unknown. At least she had physical remnants: Joshua, Hope, and Sugar. Joshua may not feel that way, but at least he was alive and uninfected. These days that was all that really mattered.

Throwing her arm over Sugar's shoulder, Mrs. Morrison scratched between her ears. Their future was a blank white space, but at least they had another day together.

Sugar sat stiffened suddenly then barked. Mrs. Morrison felt something, like a psychic tug or sorts. It was as if someone was calling for her but she couldn't make out the voice. Sugar settled back down, resting her huge head on Mrs. Morrison's chest. The feeling faded. Mrs. Morrison leaned back in her seat for the ride.

Chapter 6

EPILOGUE

ROCKS TREMBLED IN CORRIDOR Four. There were a few survivors: two humans and one *other*. The two surviving guards in Corridor Four cowered near the rubble that blocked their escape.

"Ffaammillee."

Anderson's eyes darted over to the trembling pile several feet away. He'd seen Grant get crushed under the rubble. How in the hell could he still be alive—no, animated! There was no way he could be living. Nothing human could walk away from that!

"Ffaammillee," Grant said again, louder. The rubble pulsed, moving up and down as the thing beneath it pushed.

Anderson felt around for his gun, which had fallen when the corridor caved in.

"What are you doing?" the kid next to him asked.

"I'm not sticking around for this," Anderson told him.

"What?" the kid asked.

Anderson pointed with his left, as his right hand closed around his gun.

Both Anderson and the kid watched Grant sit upright in the rubble. Grant's skull had been crushed, taking on a crescent shape. Blood and gray matter covered his face. Grant's left shoulder hung abnormally low, bone pierced the skin. Yet, as Anderson and the kid stared, Grant's bones reshaped. He pushed on his drooping shoulder, lifting it and shoving it back in place. The gray matter and blood covering his skull remained, but somehow his face filled out. The cracking and popping Anderson associated with breakage was now the music of healing.

"What the hell, man?" the kid screeched.

Anderson shook his head, then put his gun to it and fired.

Grant clutched Mrs. Morrison's locket in his hand. He ran his finger over its smooth surface. "Ffaammiillee," he rasped, then stood up and looked around. There was so much rubble in the way. He needed to recharge in order to dig his way out of it so he could find them again.

Grant's stomach growled. He inhaled, taking in the heady scent of seasoned meat. Turning his head in the direction of the scent, his eyes rested on the whimpering kid. Grant headed for him.

The kid took the gun from Anderson's lifeless hand. Trembling, the kid barely managed to put the gun to his own head. He didn't want to die. He was only nineteen years old. However, Anderson was right—he didn't want to be around for what was coming. He closed his eyes, pulled he trigger and click. Nothing.

"No. No. No. No. No," the kid chanted, as he stared at the black combat boots in front of him.

"Hungry," Grant said.

The kid screamed.

ABOUT THE AUTHOR

Meet E. M. Lacey, the caffeine-fueled architect of dark urban, dystopian, and speculative tales. With a passion for diverse adult and young adult characters, she crafts gripping narratives that linger long after the final page. When not lost in the realms of fiction, you can find her immersed in coffee memes, indulging in horror movies and anime, or exploring local comic cons and nerd gatherings.

www.emlacey.com

ALSO BY E. M. Lacey

<u>SHARED WORLDS</u>
Eldritch Trials
Song of Sin
Rise of the Elites
Trials of the Black Throne
<u>SERIES</u>
The Biggs & Myer Briefs
Biggs, Myer, and the Vampire
Spirit Box
<u>NOVELLAS</u>
A Safe Place
<u>ANTHOLOGIES</u>
Girls of Might and Magic
Kindred Kingdoms
Once Upon a Realm
Minor Mischief